Holly Surplice

Snow Still

nosy crow

Snow white.

Snow slide.

Snow chase.

Snow hide.

Snow find.

Snow still.

Snow silent.

Snow chill.

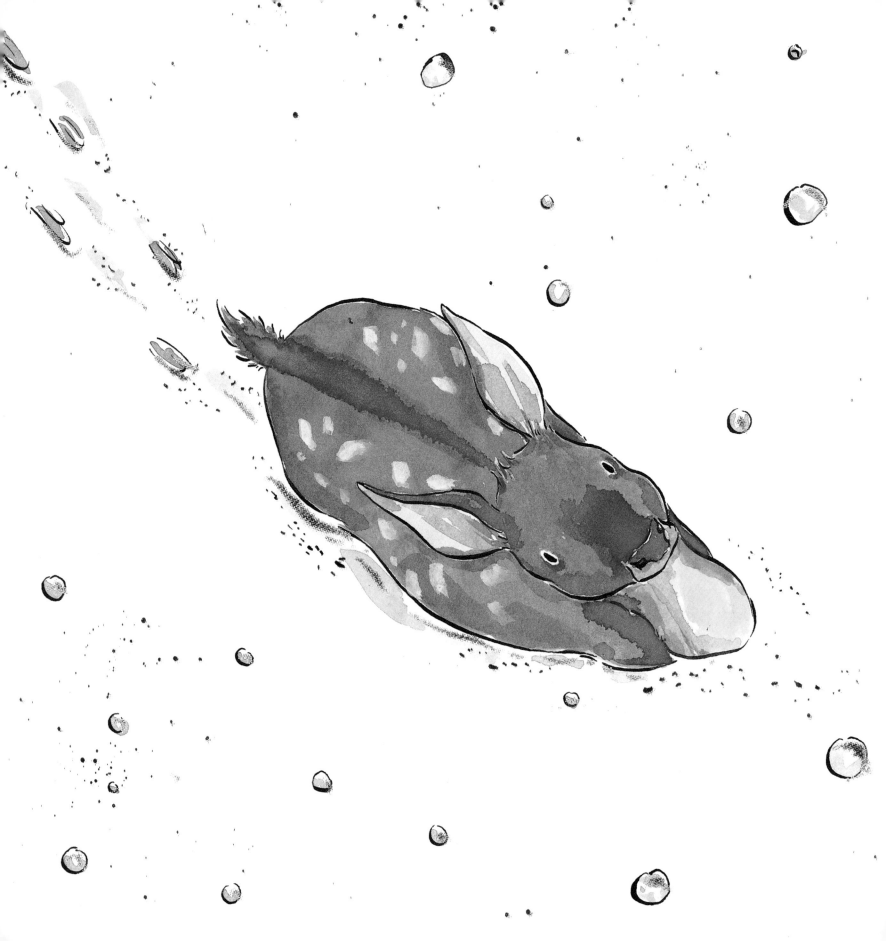

Snow fall.

Snow deep.

Snow safe,

snow sleep.

For Liz, Irwan and for Sarah

Though footprints in the snow may melt,
The warmth of love is always felt.
xxx

First published 2019 by Nosy Crow Ltd
The Crow's Nest, 14 Baden Place, Crosby Row, London SE1 1YW
www.nosycrow.com

ISBN 978 1 78800 481 7

Nosy Crow and associated logos are trademarks and/or registered
trademarks of Nosy Crow Ltd
Text and illustrations © Holly Surplice 2019

Printed in China
Papers used by Nosy Crow are made from
wood grown in sustainable forests.

1 3 5 7 9 8 6 4 2